FRANKLIN PARK PUBLIC LIBRARY

FRANKLIN PARK, IL.

Each borrower is held responsible for all library material drawn on his card and for fines accruing on the same. No material will be issued until such fine has been paid.

All injuries to library material beyond reasonable wear and all losses shall be made good to the satisfaction of the Librarian.

Replacement costs will be billed after 42 days overdue.

ASTRONAUT ANNIE

Suzanne Slade

Illustrated by **Nicole Tadgell**

TILBURY HOUSE PUBLISHERS, THOMASTON, MAINE

On Monday Annie ran all the way to her grandparents' house after school—without stopping!

She couldn't wait to tell them the news.

"What's new, Annie?" Grandpop called from the porch.

"We're having a Career Day at school on Friday," she said. "Everyone dresses up like what they want to be when they grow up."

Grandpop pulled Annie onto his lap. "How exciting! What do you want to be?"

"My teacher said to keep that a secret. But if you come to school Friday, you'll find out."

"I'll be there," he promised, locking Annie in a bear hug. "But give me a clue about what you want to be—or I'll never let you go!"

"I want," she gasped between giggles, "the whole world . . . to hear my stories."

"Of course!" Grandpop's eyes sparkled. "I have exactly what you need inside."

"I bet you want to be a reporter like me," he said, handing Annie his old camera. "You can use this for Career Day."

"I love your stories," Annie said. "On Friday you'll hear my story too."

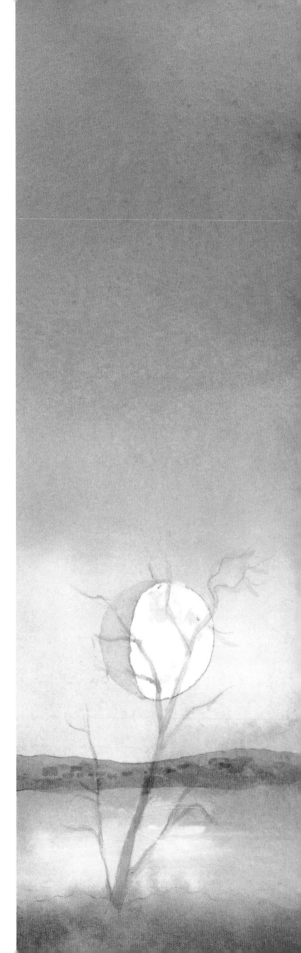

"How about a snack?"
Grandma called.

Stomach rumbling, Annie
ran to the kitchen.

"Did I hear something about Career
Day—and a secret?" Grandma asked.
"Can you give me a hint?"

"I want to be brave!" Annie said.

"Aha!" Grandma hopped to her feet.
"You want to be a bold, fearless cook
like me. Everyone loves my daring desserts!"

Grandma handed Annie her mixing
bowl and oven mitts. "You can use
these for Career Day."

Annie kissed Grandma's cheek. "You're
the bravest cook I know. On Friday,
you'll see how I can be brave too."

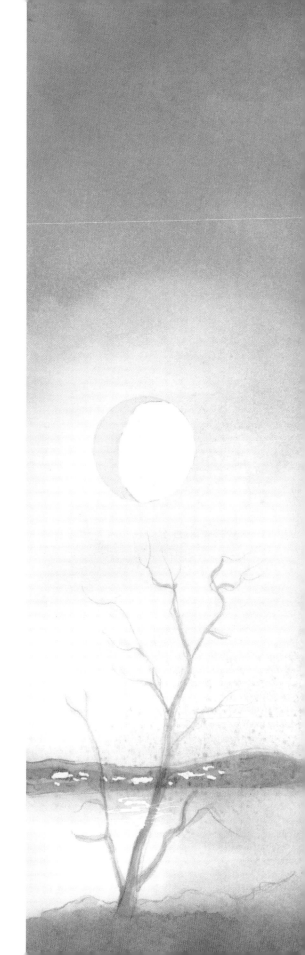

That evening Annie told her parents the news.

After dinner Dad called her into the garage. "Could you give me a clue for Career Day?" he whispered.

Annie smiled mysteriously. "I want to explore far-off places."

"I knew it!" Dad began digging through a pile of boots, maps, and water bottles. "You must want to be a mountain climber."

"I've dreamed of climbing Mount Everest for years," he said, handing Annie a large backpack. "You can't keep a secret from your old dad!"

"I enjoy our hikes," Annie said, "but wait till you hear about the places I want to explore."

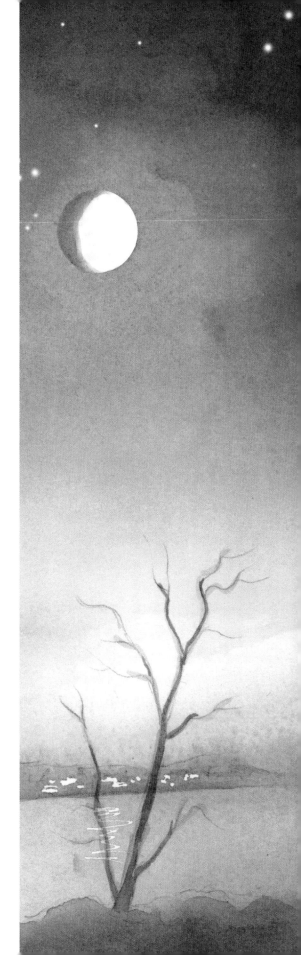

Later, Annie went outside to shoot hoops. Soon Mom joined her.

"It's so dark out here," Mom said. "Can you see the net?"

Annie stared up at the sky. "I can see lots of interesting things at night."

"How about a hint for Career Day?" Mom asked. "Just between us girls."

"I want to soar high through the air." Annie jumped and shot the ball.

Swish!

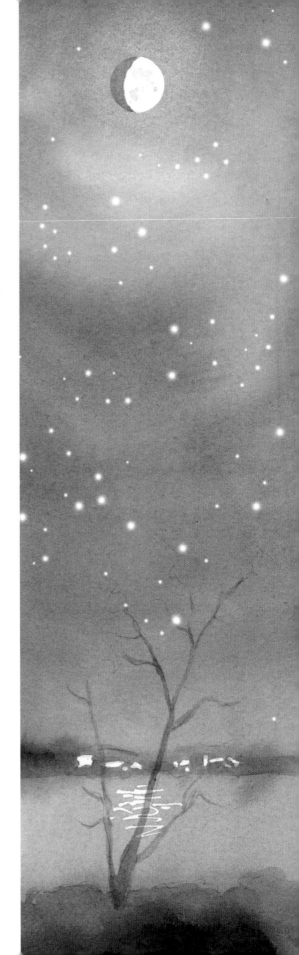

"I thought so! Wait till you see what I bought." Mom ran inside and returned with high-top sneakers. "These were on sale—and just your size."

"They're awesome," Annie said.

Annie's mom dribbled down the driveway and made a perfect layup. "I had the best time playing ball in school."

"I love basketball too," Annie said. "And on Friday you'll really see me fly."

SPACE ADVENTURES

KEEP OUT!

That week Annie worked on her costume every night.

On Friday the school buzzed with excitement. "Career Day is finally here, Annie," Dad said. "Do you feel like you're on top of the world?"

Mom scanned the packed room for empty chairs. "This is just like a crowded playoff game," she exclaimed.

"Some tasty snacks would quiet this group down," Grandma said.

Grandpop winked at Annie. "And today would make quite a news story."

Soon the teacher welcomed everyone. One by one, each student went to the front of the room to share. Finally, it was Annie's turn.

"When I grow up, I want to soar high through the air," she said, pulling on her new sneakers.

Mom flashed Annie a game-winning smile.

"And explore faraway places."
She slid Dad's backpack over
her shoulders.

Dad gave Annie a thumbs-up.

"I'll be brave and bold,"
Annie said, pulling on
her oven mitts.

Grandma's cheeks
grew round as ripe apples.

"And the whole world will hear my exciting stories." Annie slipped the camera around her neck.

Grandpop's eyes sparkled like stars.

Then Annie stood up on her chair,
put the mixing bowl firmly on her head,
and shouted, "Five, four, three, two, one . . .

BLAST OFF!"

And Astronaut Annie jumped high off her chair,
explored far-off places and soared through the air.

A famous space traveler, she was fearless and bold,
and the world loved to hear all the stories she told.

Women in Space

NASA welcomed its first class of women into the astronaut program in 1978. Since then, many brave women have followed their dreams of becoming astronauts and played important roles in space exploration missions. Here are a few of the groundbreaking women astronauts who helped make exciting new discoveries in space.

Photo c/o NASA

As a young girl, SALLY RIDE used to peer through the telescope in her bedroom window and dream about exploring space. On June 18, 1983, Dr. Ride blasted off on the *Challenger* space shuttle and became the first American woman in space. At 32 years old, she was also the youngest American ever to fly in space. She flew on a second *Challenger* mission in 1984. In 2001 she co-founded a company called Sally Ride Science, which encourages students, especially girls, to pursue science.

Photo c/o NASA

PEGGY WHITSON grew up on a large Iowa farm, but in high school she dreamed of exploring a much bigger place—space! After applying to train in the space program nine years in a row, she was finally accepted on her tenth try. In October 2007, Dr. Whitson was named the first woman commander of the International Space Station. She holds the record for the most spacewalks by a woman (ten) and has spent more time in space than any other American astronaut (655 days).

MAE JEMISON has loved science since she was very young. In kindergarten she told her teacher she wanted to be a scientist when she grew up. Dr. Jemison earned her doctorate degree in medicine in 1981. Six years later she was accepted into NASA's astronaut program. Dr. Jemison became the first African-American woman in space on September 12, 1992. She conducted many important experiments during her eight-day flight on the space shuttle *Endeavor*.

Photo c/o NASA

KATHRYN SULLIVAN enjoyed hiking and exploring nature when she was growing up. On October 11, 1984, Dr. Sullivan went on an out-of-this-world hike in space, becoming the first woman to take a spacewalk. During her long career as an astronaut, she flew on three space shuttle missions and spent more than 532 hours in space. In 2004, Dr. Sullivan was inducted into the Astronaut Hall of Fame.

Photo c/o NASA

The Magnificent Moon

Throughout history people of all ages have dreamed of exploring our beautiful moon. Only twelve humans have landed there so far, but many new, aspiring space travelers hope to visit the moon someday.

The moon is constantly circling Earth. It makes one complete revolution, or orbit, every 27 days. Because of Earth's gravitational attraction, the moon also makes one rotation on its axis every 27 Earth days. This means that the same side of the moon always faces Earth.

Half of the moon's surface is always lighted by the sun, while the other half is in darkness. How much of the lighted half we see from Earth depends on the moon's position relative to the sun and Earth. That's why the moon's glowing shape as seen from Earth keeps changing.

The moon's different shapes are called phases. The first phase is the new moon, but we can't see it! During this phase the moon is directly between the sun and Earth, with its entire lighted side facing the sun and its dark side facing Earth.

After the new moon, we see a thin sliver of moon called the waxing crescent, which grows into the first quarter moon. Then comes the waxing gibbous moon, which grows fatter each night until we see the full moon about two weeks after the new moon. Then the moon's shape begins to wane, or grow smaller. Two weeks later the new moon returns.

The moon makes a lovely nightlight for Earth. It's fascinating to watch the moon's changing phases every night!

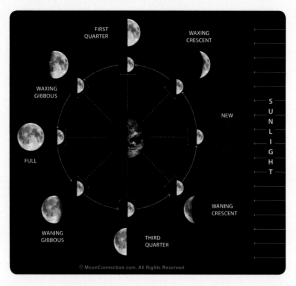
Moon's orbit around Earth

Waxing Crescent

First Quarter

Waxing Gibbous

Full Moon

Waning Gibbous

Third Quarter

Waning Crescent

Moon phase photos courtesy of NASA's Scientific Visualization Studio

SUZANNE SLADE earned a Mechanical Engineering degree and worked on Delta and Titan rockets during her engineering career. The award-winning author of 100 children's books, she enjoys writing about science and other topics. Her recent titles include *The Soda Bottle School, Dangerous Jane, The Music in George's Head*, and *The Inventor's Secret*, a 2017 "Best STEM Book" selection of the National Science Teachers Association.

NICOLE TADGELL is the illustrator of *Real Sisters Pretend* and other award-winning children's books including *First Peas to the Table, In the Garden with Dr. Carver, Lucky Beans*, and *Fatuma's New Cloth*. Her illustrations have been featured in *The Encyclopedia of Writing and Illustrating Children's Books* and in numerous exhibitions.

Sources

NASA. *Biographical Data: Sally K. Ride (PH.D.)*. Last modified July 2012. www.jsc.nasa.gov/Bios/htmlbios/ride-sk.html

NASA. *Biographical Data: Mae C. Jemison (M.D.)*. Last modified March 1993. www.jsc.nasa.gov/Bios/htmlbios/jemison-mc.html

NASA. *Biographical Data: Kathryn D. Sullivan (PH.D.)*. Last modified April 2014. www.jsc.nasa.gov/Bios/htmlbios/sullivan-kd.html

Haynes, Karima A. "Mae Jemison: Coming in From Outer Space." *Ebony Magazine*, December 1992.

Wang, Amy B. "Astronaut Petty Whitson has returned to Earth, a couple more NASA records in hand." *The Washington Post* (Sept. 5, 2017) http://wapo.st/2f0pSdr?tid=ss_tw&utm_term=.79df907c8d47

"About Dr. Sally Ride," Sally Ride Science @ UC San Diego. www.sallyridescience.com/about/sallyride/about-sallyride/

"From Iowa Farm Girl to NASA Astronaut," Buena Vista University, Sept. 8, 2009. https://www.bvu.edu/news/from-iowa-farm-girl-to-nasa-astronaut

Learn More

Anderson, Annmarie. *When I Grow Up: Sally Ride*. New York: Scholastic, 2015.

Calkhoven, Laurie. *Mae Jemison (You Should Meet)*. New York: Simon Spotlight, 2016.

Van Vleet, Carmella, and Dr. Kathy Sullivan. *To the Stars!: The First American Woman to Walk in Space*. Watertown, MA: Charlesbridge, 2016.

NASA Kids' Club. www.nasa.gov/kidsclub/index.html

NASA. *Phases of the Moon*. https://solarsystem.nasa.gov/galleries/phases-of-the-moon

TILBURY HOUSE PUBLISHERS
12 Starr Street, Thomaston, Maine 04861
800-582-1899 • www.tilburyhouse.com

Text © 2018 by Suzanne Slade
Illustrations © 2018 by Nicole Tadgell

Hardcover ISBN 978-088448-523-0

First hardcover printing January 2018

15 16 17 18 19 20 XXX 10 9 8 7 6 5 4 3

Library of Congress Control Number: 2017960120

E
470-8023

Cover and interior design:
Frame25 Productions

Printed in Korea through Four Colour
Print Group, Louisville, KY

To my dear friend
Ellen Hughes, who first
believed in Annie. —SS

For dreamers and
visionaries of all ages.
And very special thanks
to Jake, Elyce, James,
and Tristan! —NT